"Readers aren't born, they're made. Desire is planted—planted by parents who work at it."

—Jim Trelease
author of *The Read Aloud Handbook*

"When I was a classroom reading teacher, I recognized the importance of good stories in making children understand that reading is more than just recognizing words. I saw that children who get excited about reading and who have ready access to books make noticeably greater gains in reading comprehension and fluency. The development of the HELLO READING™ series grows out of this experience."

—Harriet Ziefert

Harriet Ziefert lives in Maplewood, New Jersey, and has taught children from preschool age up to 11-12 year-olds. She has written numerous books for children including NICKY'S NOISY NIGHT, NICKY'S PICNIC and WHERE'S MY EASTER EGG for very young readers, also published in Puffin Books.

Jill Bennett, who adapted the text for this edition, is a teacher specializing in primary language and works near London. She is the author of several book guides including the highly acclaimed and influential LEARNING TO READ WITH PICTURE BOOKS.

For Jamie

PUFFIN BOOKS
Published by the Penguin Group
27 Wrights Lane, London W8 5TZ, England
Viking Penguin Inc., 40 West 23rd Street, New York, New York 10010, USA
Penguin Books Australia Ltd, Ringwood, Victoria, Australia
Penguin Books Canada Ltd, 2801 John Street, Markham, Ontario, Canada L3R 1B4
Penguin Books (NZ) Ltd, 182–190 Wairau Road, Auckland 10, New Zealand

Penguin Books Ltd, Registered Offices: Harmondsworth, Middlesex, England

First published in the USA in Puffin Books, 1989
This edition published in Great Britain, 1989
1 3 5 7 9 10 8 6 4 2

Text copyright © Harriet Ziefert, 1989
Illustrations copyright © Mavis Smith, 1989
All rights reserved

Text anglicized by Jill Bennett

Printed in Singapore for Harriet Ziefert, Inc.

WHEN THE TV BROKE

Harriet Ziefert
Pictures by Mavis Smith

PUFFIN BOOKS

Jeffrey watched television
every day of the week.

Jeffrey watched on Monday...

on Tuesday...

on Wednesday...

on Thursday...

on Friday...

and on Saturday.

On Sunday
right in the middle
of a gorilla film

the TV made a loud "buzz!"
The picture faded and…

the screen went black.

Jeffrey's mum turned
all the knobs.
But nothing happened.

On Monday Jeffrey's dad
put the TV into the car.

Jeffrey sat on the sofa.

Now he had nothing to do.

On Tuesday Jeffrey asked,
"Is the TV fixed yet?"

"Not yet," Jeffrey's mum said.
"Maybe tomorrow."

On Wednesday Jeffrey said,
"It's tomorrow.
Is the TV fixed yet?"

"Not yet," she said.
"Maybe tomorrow."

On Thursday Jeffrey said
"It's tomorrow.
 Is the TV fixed yet?"

"Not yet," Mum answered.
"Maybe tomorrow."

It was Friday.

Jeffrey found some boxes.

He found paint...
scissors...crayons...
and glue, too.

"What are you doing?"
asked Jeffrey's sister.

"Nothing much," he answered.

"What are you doing now?"
asked Jeffrey's sister.

"Nothing much," he answered.

On Saturday Dad called,
"I'm home! Come and watch TV.
It's all fixed!"

"Not now, Dad," said Jeffrey.
"I'm busy. Maybe tomorrow."